WHERE THE STEPS WERE

ABBKΣ

WHERE THE
STEPS WERE

Andrea Cheng

WORDSONG

Honesdale, Pennsylvania

Also by Andrea Cheng

Marika

Honeysuckle House

The Lace Dowry

Tire Mountain

Eclipse

Brushing Mom's Hair

Text and illustrations copyright © 2008 by Andrea Cheng
All rights reserved
Printed in China
Designed by Helen Robinson
First edition

Library of Congress Cataloging-in-Publication Data

Cheng, Andrea.
Where the steps were / Andrea Cheng.—1st ed.
p. cm.
Summary: Verse from the perspectives of five students in
Miss D.'s third-grade class details the children's last year together
before their inner-city school is to be torn down.
ISBN 978-1-932425-88-8
[1. Schools—Fiction. 2. Teachers—Fiction. 3. Friendship—Fiction.
4. Novels in verse.] I. Title.
PZ7.5.C44Whe 2008
[Fic]—dc22
2007018787

10 9 8 7 6 5 4 3 2

An Imprint of Boyds Mills Press, Inc.
815 Church Street
Honesdale, Pennsylvania 18431

WHERE THE STEPS WERE

To Annette, Miss D.

FALL

DAWN
Closing Pleasant Hill

Our teacher is so tiny,
I know I weigh more,
and her name's so long
but she says just call her
Miss D.
Miss D.,
my name starts with a D too, Dawn,
like the morning.
—Good morning, Dawn.
—My grandma says
next year
they're closing Pleasant Hill
and we have to go
to Frederick Douglass.
Miss D. nods.
My grandma,
she went to Pleasant Hill,
and so did my mom,
and they turned out smart
so I don't see why
they're closing our school.
Miss D.
takes off her glasses
and looks out the window.
No matter where you go,
Dawn,
you can turn out smart.

ANTHONY
Helping

The third day
of third grade
I wake up early
and run to school
because Miss D. needs help
reaching stuff.
Good morning,
Anthony,
can you get that box for me,
please?
Inside are one hundred new pencils
with perfect pink erasers
and no points
so I sharpen twenty,
one for each of us.
Miss D. says *Anthony,*
what would I do
without you?
Nobody ever said that to me before.
Miss D.,
I have a question.
Do you spend the night
at Pleasant Hill?

JONATHAN
Welcome

I didn't even know
school started
so I missed four days.
—*Jonathan Williams?*
—*Yes, ma'am.*
—*Did you bring a note?*
—*No, ma'am.*
—*Third grade, room 103.*
In 102
the teacher is yelling
Get over here this instant
in a mad voice
like the shelter lady,
but when I get to 103
everybody's reading.
I can't find a teacher,
then this tiny lady says
Welcome, Jonathan.

KAYLA
Stone Soup

I see Grams
through the window
and run
to be the first
to give her a hug.
She reads whatever book I want
even if it's the same book
I read yesterday
because I can only read
if I already know the story.
We both like
Stone Soup
because Grams really makes soup
out of bones.
Why don't you just buy
chicken noodle
at the store,
Grams?
—Homemade soup is better.
I'll tell you what,
Kayla,
in winter I'll bring my pot
and we'll make our own
room 103 soup.

CARMEN
Grams

Grams knows even more
than Miss D.
because she's old
as Lincoln.
She's not really my grandma,
my granny passed,
she's Miss D.'s mom,
and when she was a girl
there was a war
so she had to hide
in the basement.
Was somebody
really trying to kill you?
Grams nods
and her eyes
look cloudy
like old people's,
like my granny
before she died.
I'm lucky
I don't have to hide
in our basement
because it has the biggest bugs
you've ever seen.

DAWN
Those Ears

Hey, Jonathan,
can't you get
your lazy self
up out of bed?
You walk in here
way after Grams
every single day.
You better be on time
tomorrow
because you only got
182 days left
until they blow our school up.
Miss D.
looks over at me,
she's got those ears,
so I get reading
about George Washington Carver.
You know,
you can use peanuts
for food and oil and soap.
I show Carmen
a picture in the book
of all these peanuts
that grow under the ground
and she shows me
Abraham Lincoln
who freed the slaves.

CARMEN
Time Line

Miss D. has this
long roll of paper
and we write the years
from slavery to now.
If Lincoln was alive
he'd be more than one hundred years old.
When Granny died
she was only forty-seven
but she smoked
and that made the cancer come
so now my mom's quitting
but she still smoked yesterday,
I smelled it.
It says here
Lincoln was shot
in the theater
when he was fifty-six years old.
Is that older than you,
Miss D.?
Miss D. was born
in 1956,
and we subtract from 2006,
so she's fifty,
half of one hundred,
less than fifty-six.
Was that a movie theater
where he was shot?
Miss D. says
they didn't even have movies
back then.

JONATHAN
Science Center

We take turns
mashing peanuts
in the science center
and I say *Mr. Carver*
must have got tired
of doing this
all day,
but Dawn says
If you just read the book,
you'll see
he had a whole laboratory
full of experiments.
I want to be a scientist one day
and do experiments
with electricity,
not peanuts.

ANTHONY
Church

I don't like the weekend
because church takes too long
and after church
everyone plays basketball.
I'm the tallest
but I hate that big ball
coming in my face
so I sit out
and poke a hill of ants
with a stick.
My cousin comes over and says
he hates school
and I say *I don't*
and he says *You're a nerd,
Anthony.*
I wish it was Monday
so I could help Miss D.
set up our centers.
The science center
is getting light bulbs
and batteries.
I can't wait
to see Jonathan's face
when he walks in.

KAYLA
Grounded

Dawn says
How come you're reading that same
Stone Soup *book*
again?
I say
Mind your own business
and she looks at Carmen.
At recess
Dawn and Carmen
are over by the fence.
I stay with Miss Simms,
the playground monitor,
and tell her
my brother Sy's in jail.
She talks to Mom
on the telephone
and Mom says I'm grounded
because you don't tell other people
your brother's business.
I have to stay
in my room.
My sister asks
can I watch her baby Ashley
and I say *Only in my room*
or I'll get a whipping.

Ashley sits on my lap
and I read her *Cinderella*
from the fairy-tale book
my sister got
at the library.
I know the story
from the pictures.
Ashley falls asleep.
I put her on the bed
on her stomach
the way she likes
and lie down next to her
and look at Rapunzel.
I wish I had long hair like that
so I could climb out the window.
I could visit Miss D.,
without Carmen and Dawn,
just me,
but I don't know where
her house is at
and my braids are too short.

CARMEN
A Play

We're doing *Cinderella*
in a play
like a theater,
not a movie theater.
Miss D. picks Dawn
to be Cinderella
even though Cinderella's
not supposed to be fat,
and Kayla is a stepsister
but she can't hardly read
so how's she ever going to learn
her part?
Patrice is the other stepsister
and all I get to be
is a stupid mouse.

JONATHAN
Keys

Mr. O'Leary
has all the keys,
every last one
to every last door
in our school,
even the bathrooms
and the boiler room
where he took me and Anthony
to show us
all that heat.
What's he going to do
with those keys
when they tear our school
down?

DAWN
Jelly Beans

Me and Kayla
sit on the steps
and I give her jelly beans
from my dad.
Carmen's standing by the fence
watching.
I should ask her
does she want some
but I don't feel like it
because she thinks she's all that
just because she's skinny
and now she's mad
because she's not Cinderella
or even a stepsister.

CARMEN
Meanness

Mom says
Where is Dawn?
I miss that girl.
I say
I don't
because she's Cinderella,
can you believe,
fat as she is?
And Kayla's a stepsister
when she can't hardly read.
Mom says *Carmen,*
did I teach you
that meanness?
Go to your room
and think about what you said.
I lie on my bed
and miss Granny
because she was nicer
than Mom
and she would say
It's okay, honey,
you are MY Cinderella.
I look at the picture
on the dresser
of me and Granny
sitting on the porch.
One thing I notice
is that Granny
was very, very
fat.

ANTHONY
Buckeyes

I take a box
and fill it with buckeyes
all shiny and smooth
from the big tree
in front of Pleasant Hill.
After breakfast
Miss D. says
Who has ideas
of what to do
with so many buckeyes?
Dawn says make necklaces,
Alicia says brown snowmen.
I just want to bury my hands
in the smooth coolness.
Miss D.,
when they tear down Pleasant Hill,
will they leave the buckeye tree?

DAWN
Invitations

We make invitations
to our play.
When Carmen's finished
she puts her head down
on the desk.
I look at Kayla
and we think
there she goes again,
all mad.
Then I see
Carmen's invitation says:
To Mom
and Granny in Heaven.
I wish I still had
some of those jelly beans
or something.
I write a note:
To my friend Carmen
You are the best
with a smiley face.
I fold it into
a tiny square.
Carmen opens it
and smiles a little.

JONATHAN
Batteries

You have to put the batteries in right
with the pluses and minuses
to make the bulb
light up,
see?
I can make the buzzer work
but I can't make the light and the buzzer
work at once.
Miss D. taps me
on the shoulder.
Jonathan,
before you go to the science center,
look at this messy invitation.
If somebody reads this,
will they come
to our play?
Miss D.
can't let nothing
go by
even when she knows
my mother's not coming
to any dumb play.

KAYLA
Dreams

Miss D.'s reading us a poem
by Langston Hughes,
and she has the words
on the board
so I hear her voice
and see the words,

Hold fast to dreams
For if dreams die
Life is a broken-winged bird
That cannot fly.

Hold fast to dreams
For when dreams go
Life is a barren field
Frozen with snow.

For a second
I'm reading.

JONATHAN
My Real Dream

My real dream is
that my brother
stops wetting his bed.
I can't write that.
I dream
That one day
I can have
Mr. O'Leary's keys.

KAYLA
Sy

My dream is
that Sy came home from jail
and watched our play.

CARMEN
My Turn

I dream
that we do *Cinderella* again
and I get to be
Cinderella.

DAWN
Someday

I hope my dream
comes true
so someday I can be an actress
with blond hair.

ANTHONY
Bad Dreams

I don't like dreams
when they're bad
like they cut the buckeye tree
down to the ground.

DAWN
My Eraser

Dad buys me
a soft pink eraser,
he says *Don't lose it now,*
like you did your hat,
but on Monday
it's gone.
I tell Dad
I know who stole it,
Anthony did
because he's always messing
with my stuff.
Dad marches right up
to 103
and says *Move my daughter*
away from that tall boy
who messes with her.
Miss D. says
Mr. Johnson,
I'm sorry if Anthony
borrowed Dawn's eraser
without asking.
I'll try to keep a closer eye
on things.
I stare at the floor
and there
by the coat hooks
is something pink.

It takes me forever
to go pick it up
and even longer
to walk home.
Dad says
he's not buying me anything anymore,
ever.

JONATHAN
My House

Anthony's mom
won't let me go home with him
because she doesn't know my mom
and he can't come to my house
either.
I used to have a house
before my little brother Caleb
set the mattress on fire
even though I told him
Don't play with that lighter.
He wanted to dry out the sheets
before anyone saw.

KAYLA
Barren

I ask Patrice
What does barren mean?
because she can read
better than anyone else
in 103.
—*What does what mean?*
—*"Barren field"*
like it says in the poem.
—*Baseball field.*
She pretends
to hold a bat.
Grams says *barren* means empty
like the field is empty,
like striking out,
like Pleasant Hill School
after they close it down.

JONATHAN
Our Coffee Can

We read about this girl
and there's a fire
in her apartment
just like we had
in ours.
Then she and her grandma and her mom
save up their change
in a jar.
I say *Miss D.,*
can we save our change
like that?
Anthony helps us reach
an empty coffee can.
Miss D. puts in a dime
and I add a nickel.
Anthony has a penny
so we start off
with sixteen cents.

DAWN
Being Bad

Miss D. says
it's not time to get a drink
because we're going on a field trip
to the farm
and the bus is waiting.
Patrice sneaks to the fountain
and I say *Miss D.,*
Patrice got a drink,
and she says *Dawn,*
do you enjoy
seeing other people
get in trouble?
She doesn't say one thing
to Patrice
even though she is the one
being bad.

ANTHONY
The Farm

We each get a turn
to milk the cow.
The farmer says
Squeeze from the top
and at first
nothing comes out
and then milk squirts
into the bucket.
Next we pick cucumbers
off the vines.
Farmer Otis slices them
so thin,
they're warm
on my tongue.
Finally he shows us
the apple trees.
Most of the apples
are gone
but there are a few small ones left
called Jonathans.
You think there could be apples
called Anthonys?

KAYLA
Jingles

On the way back
I sit with Carmen and Dawn on the bus,
the three of us together
making up jingles
about the stink stink stink
on the farm farm farm.
Carmen falls asleep
with her braid
touching my shoulder.
We don't care
who's Cinderella
or who reads which books
over again.

DAWN
My Notes

The thing I liked best
about the field trip
was milking the cow
and me and Kayla and Carmen
made up new jingles
on the bus.
Miss D. writes a note
on a yellow Post-it
stuck to my paper.
I'm so glad
you liked milking
the cow.
Maybe you can teach me
the jingle.
I keep the note
with the other ones
under my crayons
where nobody will get them
and they won't get lost.

CARMEN
To Farmer Otis

Dear Farmer Otis,
Thank you
for letting us
visit your farm.
P.S.
Would you like to see
our play?
It's Cinderella,
I'm a mouse,
it's on November 7
at 12:00.
Please come.

ANTHONY
Miss D.'s Son

When I get to school
it's still dark.
Me and Miss D.
sort the crayons
and test the markers.
Miss D. says
Good morning, Anthony,
real quiet.
She says her son
is in big trouble,
he got two F's
on his report card,
and her being a teacher,
that makes it so bad.
I say *Miss D.,*
I bet he'll do better
next time.
I touch Miss D.'s
smooth hair.
She takes off her glasses
and rubs her eyes.

JONATHAN
Business

Those girls,
they know everybody's business
that's not even their business.
They say
I burned down my house
and I'm homeless
like the people
under the highway
who sleep on newspaper.
I say it wasn't even me
who burned anything
and just shut
your big fat mouths.
Dawn pins me
against the wall
with her big fat arms.
Anthony pulls her
from behind
and she says
I'll tell my daddy
you were messing with me again.
Anthony lets go
and we hide
behind the dumpster.
My brother Caleb found the lighter,
I whisper
and Anthony
holds my shoulder.

DAWN
Homes

Me and Kayla and Carmen
have to do a report on homes
and we can't go out for recess
until it's done.
There are homes in the desert
where nomads live,
and igloos
at the North Pole,
and farms in Tanzania,
and in Cincinnati
some people sleep on cardboard
under a bridge
because they're homeless.

KAYLA
Harriet Tubman

Harriet Tubman didn't take no stuff
Wasn't scared of nothing neither
Didn't come into this world to be no slave
And wasn't going to stay one either.
Miss D. put that poem
on the board
and I can read
every single word
and it's my favorite poem
ever.
Harriet Tubman
didn't have no home
except the woods.
Sy doesn't have no home
except the jail.

CARMEN
Rosa Parks

Harriet Tubman,
she came before Lincoln,
but then how did Rosa Parks
fit in?
Miss Parks
just died,
Miss D. says.
—And she was a slave?
—No, she was a seamstress
who wanted to sit
in her seat on the bus.
We find 1955
on my time line.
Dang,
that was about one hundred years
after slavery.
That's one year before I was born,
Miss D. says.
—So when you were little,
we couldn't have sat together
on the bus?

KAYLA
Sy Comes Home

My brother Sy comes home,
he's so tall,
he swings me around
and holds baby Ashley
but she cries,
she wants me
instead.
Mom says *Sy,*
now you stay out of trouble
this time around.
The door opens
late at night.
Sy,
why can't you stay in?
Hold fast to dreams
For if dreams die
Life is a broken-winged bird
That cannot fly.
Harriet Tubman
Didn't take no stuff
Kayla McDonald
Didn't take no stuff
Life is a barren baseball field—
no, a barren field.
The front door clicks
and Sy's light footsteps
are on the stairs
like snow.

DAWN
Lemonade

Me and Kayla
are going to Carmen's
for lemonade
after school.
She made us invitations
with lemons on the front
and when you smell the paper
it's sour.

ANTHONY
Simon

Simon was so bad
in Ms. Jackson's class
that the principal
gave him to us.
Miss D. says it's an honor
to have Simon
join our class.
But I don't see why
we have to get the bad kids.
We told Simon
he better act right
or he's going right back
where he started from.
I saw him staring
at our coffee can
so I said
Simon,
do you have a dime
to add?

JONATHAN
Ms. Roberts

I'll be so happy
when they close Ms. Roberts' office
because she's the meanest lady
in the world,
going around in her high-heeled shoes
shouting *No talking*
into a big old horn
when she's shouting loudest
herself.
I throw one tiny piece
of orange peel
and she writes me up
so now I can't go skating.
Simon says
That's cause you're bad.
Miss D. says *Jonathan,*
next time,
are you going to throw food?

KAYLA
Suspended

Simon says
Your brother's so bad
they locked him up.
I slap Simon
on his bald head
because my brother
is none of his bald-headed business.
We both get suspended
for two days
and I have to stay
in my room.
My sister brings me grapes
and another blanket
since it's getting cold
and I tell Ashley
me and Harriet Tubman
don't take no stuff.

CARMEN
Getting Ready

I almost got to be
a stepsister
since Kayla was suspended
but when she came back
she still knew
every one of her lines.
Dawn's so fat
she can't hardly zip
the Cinderella dress
but I don't say
a word.
We have a whole crowd
come to watch our play.
Jonathan says
his mother was going to come
but she's not been feeling well
and I'm about to tell him
he's lying again
but Miss D.'s sitting right there.
Good thing your brother Caleb's class
is coming,
she says.
Then who walks in
but Farmer Otis!

ANTHONY
Cinderella!

Nobody forgot
their lines
and those stepsisters
were wicked.
You can't believe
all the clapping
in 103.
We had to come out and bow
four times
before they stopped.
Then we had cookies
Grams made
and lemonade
from Carmen's mom.
On the way out
Mr. O'Leary told me
I was an excellent prince
and he put five dollars
into our can.
I stay after
to help Miss D.
put back the chairs,
and then I count up our money,
sixteen dollars
and thirty-five cents.
Miss D.,
what are we going to do
with all that money?

WINTER

JONATHAN
Snow Day

The snow is so wet
it's soaking my shoes.
When I get to the front door
Pleasant Hill's locked.
Mr. O'Leary isn't anywhere
and neither is Miss D.
I bet she's sad
cause Miss D. hates the cold.
She wears so many sweaters
that Grams knitted her
with all that yarn
to keep her warm,
but when you touch her hands,
they're freezing.
If I knew where she lived
I'd walk over there right now
and shovel this snow
off her sidewalk
and draw her a map
to the shelter
so she could visit me
whenever she wanted
because Miss D.'s terrible
with directions.
I wait for Anthony
under the buckeye tree
but he doesn't come.
How did they all know
today was a snow day?

KAYLA
Winter Break

Ashley bites now—
see those marks on my arm?
All Christmas break
I have to watch her
so I can't go over Carmen's or Dawn's.
I wanted a *doll* baby for Christmas,
not a real one.

DAWN
Video

Mom and Dad go to work
so I stay home
and watch television
and eat popcorn
with Aunt Iris.
We watch the *Cinderella* video
I got for Christmas
but that Cinderella
has blond hair
and big eyes
with long eyelashes
and she's skinny.
I need new pants
cause I can't fasten mine
anymore.

ANTHONY
Miss D.'s Son

I get to Pleasant Hill
real early
because there's lots to do
after two weeks off.
From down the block
I see one light on
in 103.
Welcome back, Anthony.
But Miss D.'s eyes
aren't right
and I say *Miss D.,*
is it your son?
He didn't do better
yet?
—A little bit, Anthony,
but he's gone to live
with his father.
—He's not living with you
anymore?
But I know
he's coming back again
or else he's crazy.

CARMEN
Music

Miss Miller fixed our music room
like a ship
so we can sail
around the world
singing songs
from China and Mozambique.
Aaron pokes me
and says *Shhh,*
you sing too loud,
you're going to bust
my eardrums,
but Miss Miller says
I have a beautiful voice
ringing out.
Granny used to sing loud too,
all around the house.

KAYLA
Stone Soup

Grams puts water
in the pot
and sets it on the hot plate
until it boils.
Then we each get to cut up something
and put it in
like carrots and celery and beans and potatoes.
Grams puts in
a big ham bone
and I say
That's nasty,
but we make the best vegetable soup
I ever tasted
in my life.

ANTHONY
Money

While our soup's cooking
me and Jonathan and Simon count
seventeen dollars
and ninety-five cents
in the can.

JONATHAN
Apartments

Mom finds us
a new apartment
but I don't like that place
all white like a hospital
like where we took Caleb
for his wheezing
and anyway
it's too far from Pleasant Hill
to walk.
I wish I could stay with Anthony
or Miss D.
or in that boiler room
that's nice and warm.
If I got the keys
I could just sleep
in 103.

DAWN
The Substitute

Miss D.'s not in her room
or anywhere.
We don't much care
for that substitute lady.
I stand on the desk
and start dancing
and Carmen and Kayla too.
The substitute says
Ladies, please,
and Carmen and Kayla
sit right down
but for some reason
I keep on
until the principal calls
my dad.

I'm crying
and saying sorry
and scrubbing the kitchen floor.
Dad says I'm spoiled rotten,
I act bad
and lose my stuff.
He goes out
and slams the door.
My snot
goes into the bucket.

CARMEN
The Zoo

Dawn acted up
for the substitute lady
so she has to stay
with Ms. Jackson
and the bad kids
while we go
to the zoo.
We get to touch a sheep
and watch a man
shear it naked.
He gives us each a piece
of wool.
On the bus
we do *Down down baby,*
down down the roller coaster,
but it's no fun
without Dawn.
When we get back
I'll give my piece of wool
to her
because I know
me and Kayla were acting up too.
Only thing is
the principal didn't see.

DAWN
Ms. Jackson's

Miss D. left me
twenty math problems to do
in Ms. Jackson's
and I'm only on
number seven.
Dad says in summer
he's taking me to the zoo
and we're going to see the monkeys
and the polar bear
and the elephant.
But now he might
change his mind.
He's been gone
for two days.
Mom says just wait,
he'll come around.

KAYLA
Apologies

Dear Ms. Substitute,
We are sorry
we were dancing and hollering.
We will be good
next time you come.
Sincerely yours,
Kayla McDonald
Carmen DeAngelo
Dawn Johnson
P.S. We're doing fable skits next week.

Dear Miss D.,
We are very sorry
we were bad
when you were sick.
We hope
you never get sick
ever again.
Sincerely yours,
Kayla, Carmen, and Dawn

JONATHAN
Tortoise

I'm the tortoise
so I crawl real slow
but I don't stop.
Patrice is the hare,
that's like a rabbit.
She tires herself out
with all that running
and while she sleeps
I win the race.
If I really was a tortoise
I'd carry my house with me
everywhere I went
so we wouldn't need
a new apartment.

DAWN
The Boy Who Cried Wolf

Miss D. gives me
The Boy Who Cried Wolf.
He lied so much
nobody believed him
so then the wolf
ate him up.
I remember the pink eraser
on the floor
but sometimes Anthony
does mess with my stuff.

ANTHONY
The Theater

We're going downtown
to see the play
called *Aesop's Fables.*
We know all the stories
but we don't know which ones
they're going to choose.
I hope they do
The Fox and the Grapes
because that's my favorite.
The steps up to the balcony
are so steep.
Miss D. says sit back in your seat
and wait for the curtain to go up.
When the lights dim
I hold my breath
cause they shot Lincoln
in a theater.
Then this man comes up and says
somebody's spitting
on the kids below.
Miss D. whispers *It's not my children*
but he sends us back
on the bus.

JONATHAN
Not Fair

I say *Miss D.,*
that wasn't fair,
and she says
You're right, Jonathan,
but who had the power
in the theater?
—*That man,* I say.
—*I hate him,*
Dawn says.
Miss D. says
I understand,
but does that help the situation?

CARMEN
Suggestions

We're writing letters
to that man
because we had tickets to the play
and we never got to see it.
I tell him
we are very disappointed
and how does he know
who spit?
Miss D. says
offer suggestions
so I say
Give us new tickets
and do that play
over again.
P.S. We have to see the play soon
because next year
they're closing Pleasant Hill.
P.P.S. We did our own play.
It was Cinderella.

JONATHAN
The Theater Man

That theater man comes
and says he's sorry
but somebody spit.
We stand up
one at a time
and read him our letters.
Kayla reads
Why do you think it was us
who spit?
Because some of our skin is brown?
The man wipes sweat off his face
and says he'll see
what he can do.
Miss D. says *Thank you,*
we'll be waiting,
and her voice is sharp.

KAYLA
103 Poem

103 didn't take no stuff
We aren't going to a play
Not to see a single story
Send us back on the bus?
No way.

Miss D. says
How about another verse?

103 didn't take no stuff
We weren't the ones who spit
We were sitting in the dark
Waiting for the curtain
To go up up up.

I dedicate my poem
to the best teacher
in the world,
Miss D.

JONATHAN
Deposit

That apartment lady
doesn't want us
because she heard about the fire,
I don't know how.
Mom says *Jonathan,*
don't worry,
we'll find us
another one
soon as we save
the deposit.
—What's a deposit?
—It's money, Jonathan.
Maybe we can borrow
from the coffee can.

ANTHONY
Is He Home Yet?

Miss D.,
is your son come home yet?
When you take your glasses off
you don't look the same.

JONATHAN
Borrowing Money

I want to ask
can I borrow money
from the can,
but when I see Miss D. and Anthony
in the morning,
I don't ask.
I could see
if Mr. O'Leary
has five dollars.
With all those keys
he must be rich.

CARMEN
Hiding Cigarettes

Mom's coughing all the time now.
I hide her cigarettes
in the closet
but she just buys herself
another pack
and me some gum.
At night I stay awake.
I better not sleep
in case Mom can't breathe.

DAWN
More Snow Days

Two snow days in a row.
Me and Mom and Dad
walk down to the corner
and buy a box of doughnuts.
I tell Mom
Miss D. hates the cold.
Miss D. needs to put
some fat on her bones,
Mom says.
I'm thinking
she can have some of mine.

CARMEN
Hallelujah

Miss D.'s friend,
Mr. Matthews,
is an opera singer.
He comes to 103
and closes his eyes
and sings so loud,
Hallelujah, hallelujah,
hallelujah.
Simon giggles
but singing *Hallelujah*
isn't funny.
Miss D. says
Carmen, I like
the way you're listening.
I wish my granny was here
because she sang *Hallelujah* too.
Mr. Matthews,
can you please teach us
how to sing
like that
so I can be
an opera star?

KAYLA
Tests

They have all these tests
like benchmark and proficiency
but I don't even care
about those boring stories
that I can't read.
Miss D. says
You better care, Kayla.
If you don't pass
you'll have to repeat third grade.
Before the test
Miss D. puts the dreams poem
back on the board.
and then I remember
I can read.

DAWN
Looking Decent

That test
has a dumb story
about a girl
who doesn't have any clothes on
in the picture.
Miss D. says she does,
that's called a leotard,
but I still think
they drew her naked.
On my test I write
I don't think you should give us
this kind of test
unless you have that girl
looking decent.

CARMEN
The Hospital

Hallelujah,
the tests are done.
Grams brings us cookies
to celebrate
even though we don't know
who passed.
Then the principal
comes to the door
and says something to Miss D.
They call me over
and Miss D. says
Carmen,
your aunt Mary is coming
to pick you up today.
Aunt Mary? She lives
over in Indiana.
Miss D. holds my hand.
Your mother is in the hospital.
I suck in my breath.
My granny died there.

SPRING

KAYLA
Get Well

We all write
get-well cards
to Carmen's mom.
I write a poem:
Please don't stay sick
Now it's spring
The flowers are coming.
I draw red flowers
on the front.

CARMEN
Oxygen

Mom comes home
with this oxygen tank
and a tube to her nose.
It's hard to talk
so we just watch TV.
Then Dawn and her mom come
with a big ham,
potatoes,
and green beans.
Aunt Mary eats
but Mom and me,
we aren't hungry.

ANTHONY
Slogan

This time
the principal picks me
to say the slogan
to the whole school.
She gives me the horn
and I shout
At Pleasant Hill School
all students can meet or exceed
all defined expectations
and apply those standards
to everyday life.
—Miss D.,
I said it perfect,
didn't I?
I sound just like a white boy now,
don't I?
—You sound like a boy
who memorized the slogan,
Anthony.

JONATHAN
Another Apartment

Anthony's voice
is too loud
in that horn
like the shelter lady.
She says we've been there long enough.
Mom found a place
but the bathroom is down the hall.
That's not good for Caleb,
he'll wet his pants
for sure,
and anyway,
we still need the deposit.
Mom says *Jonathan,*
you are never satisfied.

CARMEN
Bravery

We learn about the Civil War
and Jim Crow
and Rosa Parks
and Martin Luther King.
I say *Miss D.,*
there aren't too many white kids here.
Simon says white kids are scared
to walk down our street.
That Rosa Parks,
she sure was brave
not to give up her seat.
We each get to write
about when we were brave.
Anthony says
when he rode the King Cobra,
I say
when Mom's oxygen ran out
and I called the oxygen lady
myself.

KAYLA
Merry-Go-Round

The new poem is about
a merry-go-round.
The boy is supposed to sit in the back
because of Jim Crow.
Why didn't he?
asks Miss D.
I shoot up my hand.
Because he was brave.
Then Patrice says
there's no back
to a merry-go-round.
That girl is so smart
and so was Langston Hughes.

ANTHONY
Buds

The sun is warm
on my back.
The buckeye tree
has fat buds.
Jonathan says one bud
has one leaf
but I don't know.
We have to be patient
like the tortoise.
Wait and see.

DAWN
Homework Together

Mom's going to school
just like me
so someday
she can be a nurse.
We do our homework together
at the kitchen table.
Dad says what a shame
we're both going to be smarter
than him.
His shoulders are hunched
and I hug him
around his legs
and say *No way*
because my dad beats everyone in chess
at the park
and he catches fish
even when they're not biting.
Good thing he came home
after five days.
I wonder where he stayed.

KAYLA
Teaching Ashley

My sister's so smart,
she reads these fat books
from the library
but she never did graduate
because she had Ashley.
Now I'm teaching Ashley
the ABC song
so she can get smart
but by the time she's in kindergarten
there won't be one brick left
of Pleasant Hill.

ANTHONY
Buckeye Leaves

Guess what,
Miss D.,
the buds opened!
We hurry over
and there's twenty-five
baby leaves
in one bud,
can you believe that?
I wonder how many buckeyes
there'll be.
When they tear down Pleasant Hill
they better leave this tree.
We can plant buckeyes
at Douglass,
Miss D. says.
Then we'll have
baby buckeye trees
all over the place.
I never even thought
buckeyes were seeds.

JONATHAN
Everything Dies

Grams had a husband once
and so did my mom
but their husbands died.
Everything dies
like these cicadas
all over the playground.
Simon's dad
was murdered one day
and so was Lincoln
in that theater
and Martin Luther King
talking about dreams.

ANTHONY
Cicadas

Miss D. says
don't even touch
the cicadas
but Jonathan picks one up
and puts it down Dawn's back
because he's tired of her
always making up stories
about us.
She goes hollering
and the security guard says
Hit him for that.
Dawn pulls back
her big fat arm
and I grab it
from behind.
Miss D.
pokes her head
out the window.
Jonathan and me run
behind the dumpster.

DAWN
Saying Sorry

I tell Miss D.
that the security guard
told me to hit.
Do you always listen
to other people?
What if they tell you
to jump off the bridge
into the Ohio River,
are you going to do it?
I shake my head.
Even grown-ups
can be wrong,
Dawn.
We all have to say sorry
to each other,
but the security guard
doesn't have to say
a thing.

KAYLA
Down Down Baby

Dawn and Carmen and me
sit on the concrete steps
by the gym
and clap our hands
up and down
on our knees
so fast
our hands fly.
Down down baby,
down down the roller coaster.
My sister says
she's going to take us
to King's Island this summer
and we can ride
The Beastie,
but I think I might be too scared
and somebody has to stay
with Ashley.

ANTHONY
Sitting in the Sun

Miss D.?
She doesn't hear me,
sitting there by herself
with the sun across her face.
I wish I could
find Miss D.'s son
and drag him home
where he belongs.

CARMEN
Teaching Miss D.

Miss D.,
you want us to teach you
how to clap?
We go real slow
but her hands still tangle.
She says she's too old
but I think
she's just not paying attention.

DAWN
Sorting Change

We sort the change
in the coffee can
into piles
of quarters and dimes and nickels and pennies
and one
Sacagawea dollar.
We count up each pile
and Patrice writes
15.25 and 2.30 and 1.65 and 1.35
on scrap paper.
We add up the columns
and carry
and get twenty dollars and fifty-five cents,
but we forgot the five dollars
from Mr. O'Leary
so it's twenty-five.
Miss D.,
you think twenty-five dollars
and fifty-five cents
is enough
to buy this old building
ourselves?

JONATHAN
I'm Not Going

Mom picked the apartment
without even showing it to me first
and I bet she still doesn't have
that deposit.
I might just not go
if I have to change schools.
I might stay at the shelter.

CARMEN
Talent Show

Mom can't hardly talk
with all that oxygen
so me and Kayla and Dawn
write her notes
on the porch.
She smiles
when she reads them.
Then she takes a nap
and we move inside
cause if we can't hear her breathing
we get scared.
We practice
a talent show
with singing and dancing.
After a while
Mom opens her eyes and whispers
Sing me that pretty
Hallelujah song.

ANTHONY
Hot

Somebody took
the five-dollar bill.
Miss D. says
she's so disappointed
and would whoever borrowed it
please put it back.
It's so hot
we stick to the chairs.
The fan is blowing
our papers around.
Miss D. says
Let's get to work.

JONATHAN
Pizza

I almost give Mom the money
but she might say
Jonathan,
where'd you get that five dollars?
Me and Caleb
buy a pizza
and eat it so fast
and drink the pop.
There's fifty cents left
so we get a cookie
and split it.
Mr. O'Leary won't mind
about his five dollars
long as I pay it back.

KAYLA
Scrapbook

We're making a scrapbook
of our year.
Everyone gets one page.
I bring a picture of Ashley
and I draw me
right beside her
reading books
on the bed.
I don't even put Sy in there
because he left
and Mom says this time
she's not letting him
come home.
On the back
I write him a poem:
Sy, please be good
good good
because I miss you
you you.

ANTHONY
My Picture

I draw buckeyes
covering my page.
Dawn says *Anthony,*
can't you draw something
better than that?
I say
Is it your business?

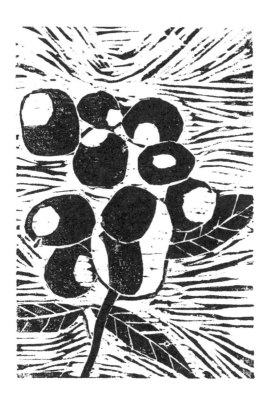

CARMEN
Secret Ballot

School's almost out.
We have to spend the money
somehow.
We put suggestions
on the board:
Pizza party.
Roller skating.
How about thinking
of other people?
Miss D. says.
Kayla raises her hand.
A present for Grams,
she says.
What would Grams like?
I put my head down
and shut my eyes
and think.
A big picture of us
in front of Pleasant Hill,
I say.
We vote
on slips of paper
called secret ballots.
Pizza gets four,
skating gets three,
and the picture wins.

JONATHAN
Say Cheese

I wish I had
a camera like that
with a flash
on top.
Mr. O'Leary
lines us all up
in front of the school
with Miss D.
right in the middle.
Say bunny rabbit
with cheese,
he says.
We laugh
and he clicks.

ANTHONY
Summer Plans

We're supposed to write
our summer plans.
My summer plan
is to visit Miss D.
but I don't know where
your house is.
I hope it's close
to vacation Bible school
because that's where I'll be
every single day.
Sincerely yours,
Anthony

KAYLA
Writing

My name is Kayla.
This summer
I want to write poems.
Do you know the one
about the merry-go-round?
That's my favorite.

JONATHAN
Thank You for a Good Year

Our principal says
Thank you for a good year
and have a good summer
but I won't
because Mom got the deposit
and from my new apartment
I can't even walk to Pleasant Hill.
Every single day I'll be wondering,
is today the day
they're coming with the bulldozer?
Anthony says
it'll take more than one
for sure
and a backhoe
to get that boiler out.
When Pleasant Hill School is gone,
I wonder,
can I have all those keys?

DAWN
Our Last Day

We don't feel much like talking
except Simon.
He always talks too much.
I wish he would've stayed
in Ms. Jackson's.
He says
I don't like
this old school.
The closet has a leak
and the bricks are falling down
and at Douglass
they have air conditioning,
did you know that?
Simon,
since this is our last day,
can you please
keep your mouth
shut?

JONATHAN
Next Year

Next year
at Douglass
I'll find Miss D.,
and when she's not looking
I'll put five dollars
into the coffee can.

CARMEN
Finding Miss D.

I won't know
where to find Miss D.
in Douglass.
I'll find you,
she says.
Now I have to worry
all summer
because Miss D.,
she's terrible at directions
like left and right.

KAYLA
The Barren Can

The picture cost ten dollars.
With the rest of the money
we got a frame
that has real glass.
Grams keeps looking at that picture
and smiling.
I don't care
if our coffee can is barren.

ANTHONY
Bookworms

Grams gives each of us
a bookworm
out of yarn
that she made herself.
I know
because the yarn
matches Miss D.'s sweater.
Miss D. gives us a pencil
with part shaved off
where she wrote our names
and a card
with a small picture
of us in front of Pleasant Hill
and a special note
for each of us.
On mine she writes
Dear Anthony,
What would I do without you
every morning?
Miss D.

DAWN
Dear Miss D.

Dear Miss D.,
I loved Cinderella,
that was my favorite thing.
The worst was
we couldn't see that play,
we never even knew
which fable they picked.
That man said
he was going to get us tickets
but he lied
like the boy who cried wolf.
Love, Dawn.

CARMEN
Promises

Dear Carmen,
I'm so bad at finding things
but next year,
I'll find you,
I promise,
Miss D.
Miss D.
always
keeps her promise
and I'll
always
keep
my
note.

JONATHAN
Please

The new apartment
is far away.
Please ask Mr. O'Leary
to leave the keys
with the shelter lady
and I'll stop back
and pick them up.

ANTHONY
P.S.

P.S. Your son is definitely coming home THIS summer.

KAYLA
The Steps

Dear Miss D.,
Me and Carmen and Dawn
will meet you and Grams
on the steps of Pleasant Hill
in the morning
the first day of school,
and if the steps
are gone
we'll meet you
where they were,
and we'll walk you
all the way
to Douglass.
Love,
Kayla